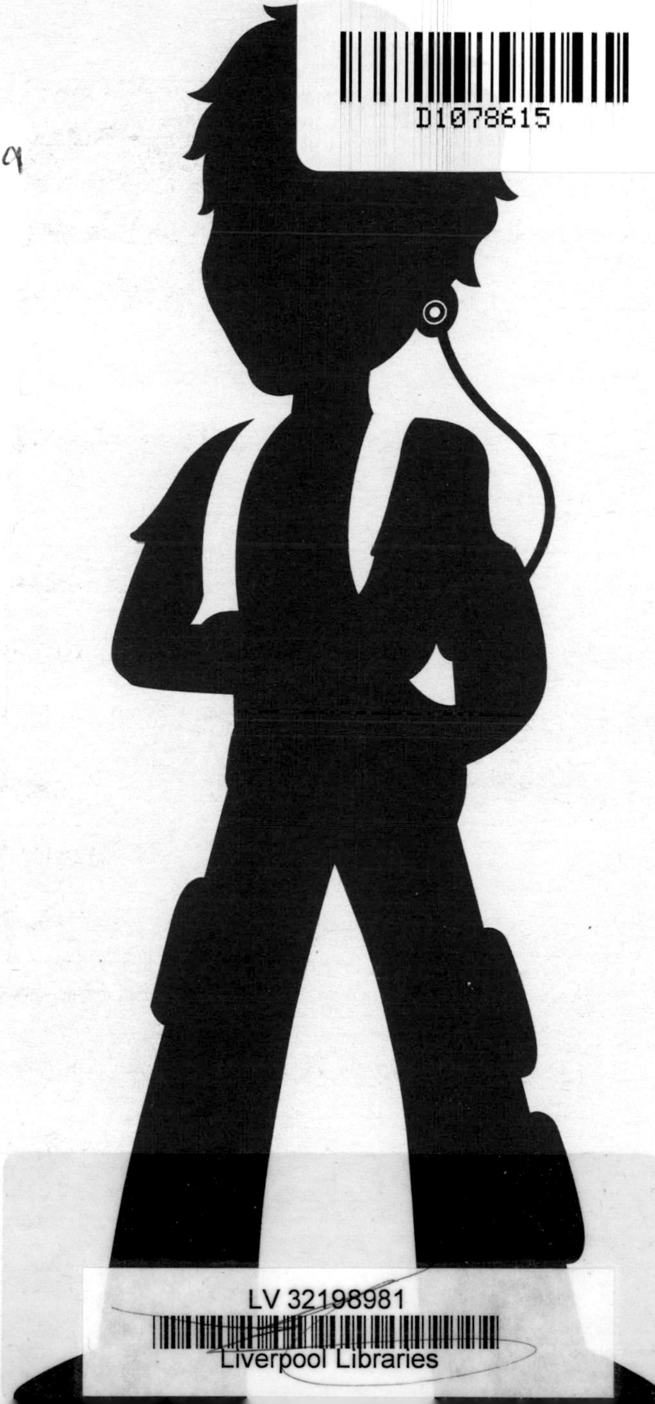

Follow Zac's other adventures in:

Poison Island
Deep Waters
Mind Games
Frozen Fear
Night Raid

For your spy name, downloads
and other Zac Power info, go to
**www.zacpower.com**

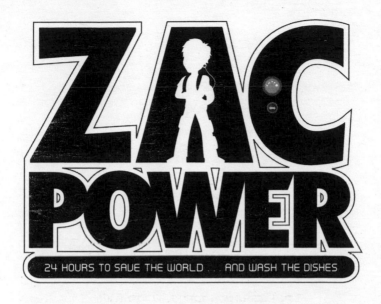

# TOMB OF DOOM

## BY *H. I. LARRY*

### ILLUSTRATIONS BY
### *ASH OSWALD & ANDY HOOK*

**EGMONT**

# EGMONT

*We bring stories to life*

First published in Australia 2006
by Hardie Grant Egmont
This edition published 2007
by Egmont UK Limited
239 Kensington High Street
London W8 6SA

Text copyright © H. I. Larry 2006
Illustrations and design copyright © Hardie Grant Egmont 2006

The moral rights of the author and illustrator have been asserted

ISBN 978 1 4052 3097 1

1 3 5 7 9 10 8 6 4 2

A CIP catalogue record for this title is available
from the British Library

Printed and bound in Great Britain by the CPI Group

# CHAPTER ...ONE

*Sometimes,* thought Zac Power, *being a spy isn't as cool as it sounds.*

Right now he was on a camel in the middle of the desert. Zac knew that this might sound good to another kid. But it really wasn't.

For one thing Zac's camel kept spitting gross stuff onto his sneakers. Then there was the heat. The sand was so hot that if you were dumb enough to walk on it without shoes your feet would melt up to your ankles — just like butter on hot toast.

The heat was terrible for Zac's hair, too. He had already used half a tube of Super-Strength Hair Gel.

The other reason this trip wasn't cool was that his entire family was here too. Everyone in the Power family was a spy, even Zac's geeky brother Leon.

They all worked for the Government Investigation Bureau, or GIB for short. Zac had been on some awesome missions, but this family holiday wasn't one of them.

Zac tried to pass the time by playing the latest game on his SpyPad.

SpyPads look like game consoles. But they are actually mini-computers, with a mobile satellite phone, a laser and a code-breaker too.

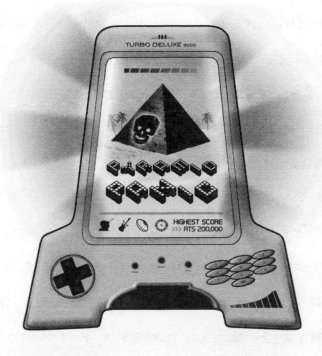

Zac was usually excellent at electronic games, but this one had him stumped.

It was called *Pyramid Panic*. Whenever he reached the treasure room in the middle of the pyramid he was ejected out through a hole in the roof. Zac's highest score so far was 2000. One player called A.T.S. had the top score of 200,000! *Dumb game,* thought Zac, as he deleted it from his SpyPad.

The tour guide on the front camel was droning on.

'We are now entering the desert region of the Amber Sands. The famous Vanishing Pyramid which is the tomb of the Golden Sun King is said to be located here,' he said. 'It's the only pyramid never to be looted by tomb raiders.'

'That's because it's guarded by GIB,'

Leon whispered to Zac. 'Apparently it's stuffed full of treasure.'

'According to legend,' continued the guide, 'if the Vanishing Pyramid is ever broken into terrible earthquakes will shake the Amber Sands. The locals call the pyramid the Tomb of Doom ...'

As he spoke something really strange happened. The earth began to tremble.

**RRRRRUMMMMBLE!**

The tour guide went pale.

'Let's all stop here,' he said nervously. But Zac's camel wouldn't stop. With a snort it turned and galloped away from the group.

'Bye, sweetie!' called his mum. 'Don't forget to wear your hat!'

The camel galloped faster and faster. And faster. And *faster!* It went so fast that smoke started streaming out of its nose.

*Smoke?* thought Zac. *That can't be right...*

Then he noticed a metal plate attached to the camel's neck, hidden by fur.

CAMELTRONIC 9000.

Zac had heard about this from Leon. It was a state-of-the-art robot with ten gears and airbags. Zac wished he'd realised this earlier – the CAMELTRONIC had a drinks dispenser in its hump!

Had GIB arranged for this camel to take him to his next mission? There was nothing Zac could do but wait and see ...

On and on the camel ran until finally

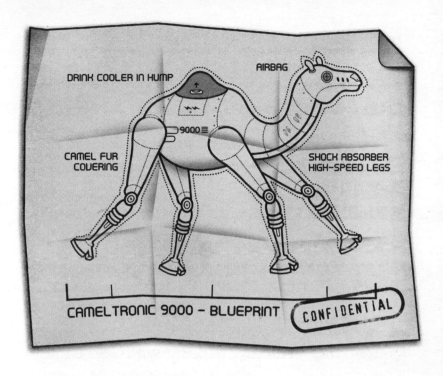

**DRINK COOLER IN HUMP**

**AIRBAG**

**9000**

**CAMEL FUR COVERING**

**SHOCK ABSORBER HIGH-SPEED LEGS**

CAMELTRONIC 9000 – BLUEPRINT  CONFIDENTIAL

they reached an oasis. The camel groaned and collapsed in a heap beneath a palm tree. Zac quickly jumped off and looked around. There was nothing there except a pond and the palm tree.

Zac had been hoping that he was about

to be sent on some cool mission. But that was clearly a false alarm. Disappointed, Zac kicked the palm tree.

'Stop that,' said the tree, crossly.

Zac looked closer and saw that the tree was actually GIB Agent Peterson in disguise. Agent Peterson shook one of his leaves and a date fell onto the sand.

'Eat that,' he commanded.

Zac bit carefully into the soft flesh. He suspected that this wasn't a normal date. Sure enough, his teeth hit something hard. Zac spat out a metal disk.

All right! His next mission!

Zac loaded the disk into his SpyPad.

...loading...

# CLASSIFIED
## MISSION RECEIVED 2.00PM

Top GIB spy, Agent Track Star, is MIA while guarding the Vanishing Pyramid. Tremors have rocked the Amber Sands region, which means the pyramid has been entered. Raiders may have broken into the tomb, and GIB now fears Agent Track Star is trapped inside.

### YOUR MISSION

- Locate and enter the Vanishing Pyramid.
- Find and/or rescue Agent Track Star.
- Repair any damage done to the pyramid.

### SPECIAL NOTE

If anyone remains inside the Vanishing Pyramid 24 hours after the tremors first start, the pyramid will collapse.
Anyone inside will be trapped forever!

### END

SUNSCREEN MODE
>>> ON

Just then, the ground shook again.

Zac turned to Agent Peterson.

'When did these tremors start?' he asked urgently.

'About two hours ago,' replied Agent Peterson. 'Just after Agent Track Star went missing.'

Right. Zac knew he had to click into action. He looked at his watch.

If Agent Track Star had already been inside the pyramid for two hours, that meant he had until midday tomorrow ...

Zac was already behind time!

# CHAPTER... ...TWO

Zac wanted to set off straight away. But there was one small problem. The CAMEL-TRONIC 9000 was in no state to go anywhere. Luckily Agent Peterson seemed to know what Zac was thinking. He shook his leaves again and a set of keys fell into Zac's hands.

At first Zac didn't know what the keys were for. Then he spotted a cool looking car behind Agent Peterson. It was painted a sandy colour so it blended in with the desert. It had a roll bar instead of a roof and on the back was a big solar panel.

Awesome! A solar-powered dune buggy!

Zac jumped in and started it up.

'There's a Pyramid-Pack in the back that Agent Tech Head put together for you,' said Agent Peterson. 'It's full of useful gadgets for a mission like this.'

'Great,' said Zac. 'Now, which way do I go?'

'North, I think,' replied Agent Peterson. 'Or maybe east.' He didn't sound very sure.

*I'll head north-east,* decided Zac as he revved the engine and set off. It was strange

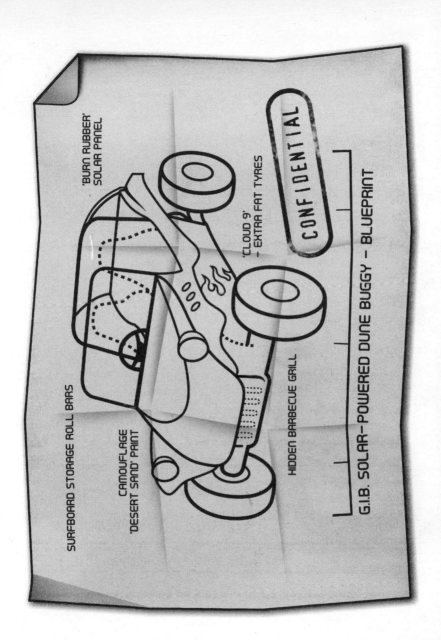

'BURN RUBBER' SOLAR PANEL

'CLOUD 9' – EXTRA FAT TYRES

CONFIDENTIAL

SURFBOARD STORAGE ROLL BARS

CAMOUFLAGE 'DESERT SAND' PAINT

HIDDEN BARBECUE GRILL

G.I.B. SOLAR–POWERED DUNE BUGGY – BLUEPRINT

not having proper directions but Zac wasn't worried. Surely it couldn't hurt to go for a short joy-ride first!

The dune buggy was excellent. It zipped around palm trees and screeched around boulders. Zac even drove it on two wheels. Then he flew over the sand dunes, making huge sand clouds behind him as he bounced back down on the big fat tyres.

After a while, Zac started getting hungry. Was there any food in the buggy? Zac couldn't find any. But then he noticed a button on the dashboard with a picture of a hamburger on it. Curiously, Zac pushed it. With a whirr the buggy's bonnet folded up. Underneath was a barbecue grill.

As Zac watched, the left windscreen wiper slapped a meat patty onto the sizzling grill while the right wiper chopped up lettuce and tomatoes. Ten minutes later Zac was eating a delicious burger. There were even some chips on the side.

The dune buggy's clock beeped.

He'd been on this mission for two hours and didn't even know where he was heading yet. Time to talk to Agent Tech Head.

'Hi, Leon,' said Zac when his brother's

face appeared in the SpyPad's satellite phone screen. 'Any idea where to find this Tomb of Doom?'

'I haven't been able to find the exact location,' Leon admitted, 'but I'll send you what I know. There are some sunglasses in the Pyramid-Pack. Put them on.'

The sunglasses were much less stylish than the ones Zac was already wearing. But when he put on them on he understood why Leon wanted him to wear them.

Head Up Display sunglasses!

Any information Leon sent was beamed directly onto the inside of each lens.

Leon sent through a message straight away.

The Vanishing Pyramid is located somewhere around 27.66° latitude and 28.25° longitude.

Zac entered the coordinates into the SpyPad's GPS. Then Leon sent another message.

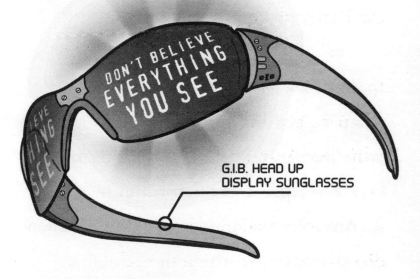

G.I.B. HEAD UP
DISPLAY SUNGLASSES

What did that mean?

But there was no time to wonder.

Zac had to keep going. He found his favourite driving music on his iPod: Jet's *Get Born*. Then he slipped the buggy into cruise control and settled back. He still had a long way to drive.

The sun was setting when Zac finally spotted a building on the horizon. That *had* to be the Vanishing Pyramid! Zac jammed his foot on the accelerator. But instead of speeding up, the dune buggy slowed down and then stopped altogether.

Zac looked at the battery meter and groaned. He was out of solar power! He was going to have to make the rest of the journey on foot.

Even though it was evening the sand was still burning hot. When Zac tested it with the tip of his sneaker it instantly started turning into goo. There was no way Zac could walk across here!

Quickly he checked the Pyramid-Pack. In it he found a pair of daggy sandals and some white knee-high socks. Zac put the socks back straight away. There was *no way* he was wearing socks and sandals. That was something Leon would do!

But Zac took a closer look at the sandals. They were Track Changers. A dial on the side of each shoe allowed him to choose

what kind of animal prints he wanted them to make. He didn't need to disguise his footprints but Zac slipped the shoes on anyway. He remembered from spy training that Track Changers were heat-proof!

Zac chose 'Camel' and headed towards the Vanishing Pyramid.

# CHAPTER ...THREE

Zac trudged through the moonlight for what felt like hours until the pyramid was just up ahead. And then the Vanishing Pyramid ... vanished!

'Whoah!' said Zac. 'Where did it go?' He spun around and there it was behind him. Zac ran towards it. But when he got close the pyramid disappeared again. It reappeared a few moments later in a new spot. Then Zac remembered Leon's final message: *Don't believe everything you see.*

Could there be some kind of mirage generator protecting the pyramid? Zac knew that mirages often looked so real that people imagined they could see water when there was nothing but hot air. Perhaps that was what was happening now.

Zac needed a way of telling the difference between the real and the imaginary. Then he remembered the latest plug-in that he had downloaded for his SpyPad: the Mirage Filter.

He switched the SpyPad into Mirage Filtering mode. When he held it up to the pyramid that kept disappearing, all he

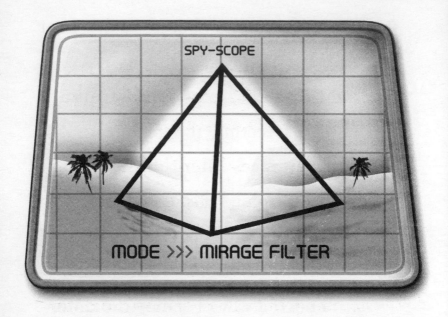

could see was an outline. This meant that
the pyramid was a mirage.

Then Zac scanned around the desert
and a pyramid appeared clearly on the
screen in area where there was nothing to
see at all. Zac smiled. That had to be the
real Vanishing Pyramid!

Zac checked his watch.

He'd wasted a lot of time chasing mirages. Better get moving.

Zac raced towards the true location of the Vanishing Pyramid. At first he couldn't see anything. But as he got closer the Vanishing Pyramid began to appear, like it was coming out of a fog. The closer Zac got the more solid it became.

Finally the pyramid was right in front of him. Zac reached out his hand. It was a big relief to feel the solid rock beneath his fingers.

But now Zac faced a new problem.

*How do I get in there?*

He walked around the outside looking for clues. Halfway around he saw some hieroglyphics and his spy senses started tingling. Maybe this would tell him how to get in.

Zac had a pretty good idea what the symbols might mean. But just to be sure he switched his SpyPad into Code-Breaking mode and scanned it along the rock.

Seconds later, the SpyPad flashed the decoded message up on screen.

Knock before entering.

Could it be that simple to get into the pyramid? It didn't seem possible.

*Well, it can't hurt to try,* thought Zac. He rapped sharply on the rock.

Instantly it slid away to reveal a dark cavern. Zac stepped inside. With a thud the rock slid back into place and Zac found himself in total darkness. Time to switch the SpyPad into Glow mode.

Once he had some light Zac looked around. What he saw took his breath away.

The walls around him were covered in paintings. One painting showed a room full of glittering jewels. Another painting was of enormous snakes. There was also a painting of people being chased by huge scorpions.

In front of Zac were three golden doorways, each decorated with precious stones. Behind them were three tunnels leading off into the darkness. He was at the start of a maze!

*Agent Track Star must have gone down one of these*, thought Zac. *But which one?*

Zac knew that lots of pyramids were filled with booby traps and false passages. Were the paintings a warning of what lay ahead? Zac didn't like the look of the snakes or the scorpions.

Which way should he go?

# CHAPTER... ...FOUR

*Better speak to Leon again,* decided Zac. But the thick walls of the pyramid made it hard to get a clear signal. Leon's face appeared fuzzy on the screen of his SpyPad and his voice kept dropping out.

'Play the game,' was all that Zac could hear. It wasn't like Leon to talk about games during a mission.

'*Pyramid Panic,*' Leon finally yelled before

the signal dropped out.

*Pyramid Panic*? That stupid game that Zac had deleted from his SpyPad? Why was Leon telling him to play that when he wanted help through this maze?

*Hang on,* thought Zac. *The maze in* Pyramid Panic *must be the same as the one inside the Vanishing Pyramid!*

The more he thought about it the more sense it made. GIB probably made the game as a way of disguising what they knew about the inside of the Vanishing Pyramid. That way if a SpyPad ever fell into enemy hands they wouldn't even realise what the game really was.

It was a clever idea. But there was one

slight problem. Zac didn't have the game any more. He was going to have to rely on what he could remember.

Zac looked at the three entrances and thought about the last time he'd played *Pyramid Panic*. The left-hand passage led to a dead end. And he was pretty sure the right-hand one ended up in a deep hole. He knew that because he'd fallen into it a couple of times.

Easy! That only left the middle passage.

As he headed off into the dark tunnel Zac noticed something scratched into the ground.

Zac smiled — he didn't need his SpyPad to solve this clue.

His school project on Egypt had taught him enough to work out the letters ... GIB.

*My hunch was right*, he thought. *Agent Track Star must have gone this way!*

Just then the ground rumbled and the walls shook. Zac set off again at a brisk pace. There was no way he was getting stuck in here!

After walking for hours Zac stopped to check the time.

This didn't feel like the right way any more. *I'll keep going for a bit longer*, Zac thought, taking a step forward. And then the ground disappeared!

Zac plunged into a deep hole. As he landed his head whacked against the side of the hole.

Instantly, Zac was knocked out.

He wasn't sure how much time had passed when he finally came round. But losing any time at all was bad. *Great*, Zac thought, annoyed. *How do I get out?*

It was very dark in the hole. He felt around for his SpyPad to get some light. But it wasn't there! He must have dropped it in the passage above when he fell.

This was just like playing *Pyramid Panic*, but worse. At least with the game he could turn it off and start all over again when things went bad.

Zac felt the walls around him. They were very slippery and steep. If only he had some sort of light! It was impossible to do anything in this darkness.

Zac looked down and saw a bluish light moving around the floor. He blinked a few times but the light was still there. A moment later it was joined by other blue lights. Soon there were enough lights for Zac to see what was going on.

The crawling lights were beetles with big horns. Each one was the size of Zac's palm and had wings that glowed with a purple light. They looked familiar to Zac, but where from?

Oh yeah! Ultraviolet Glowing Scarab Beetles – Zac had seen them on Leon's favourite nature show – *Creepy Creatures*.

Then Zac had a brilliant idea. He fished out the ugly knee-high socks from the Pyramid-Pack. Then he carefully scooped up the beetles and put them in the sock.

**SCARABAEUS LUMINUS**

**CREEPY CREATURES**

Ultraviolet glow-emitting beetle,
worshipped by the ancient Egyptians.

Before long the sock was glowing as
brightly as a torch. The beetles wriggled a
lot but Zac tied a knot in the end so they
couldn't escape.

*Don't worry,* he promised them. *I'll let you
go later.* Then he held up the sock-torch to
have a look around.

On the side of the hole he saw another carving:

This was nothing that he'd learnt at school and he didn't have his SpyPad decoder with him. *I'll just have to work it out for myself*, Zac realised.

He looked carefully at the pictures. The first one was obviously a door. The second one was a figure with its finger to its lips – it looked like his mum when she wanted him to be quiet or when something was a secret. *Maybe there's a secret exit around here?* thought Zac.

Zac shone the torch around and there in the ground was a small hook. He pulled it, and instantly a rock slid back in the wall to reveal a passage leading up. It was very narrow. Zac would have to wriggle through it on his stomach. And what if it didn't lead back up to the main passage? He was just going to have to risk it.

But Zac knew this was probably the only way out of this hole. He was going to have to just risk it.

# CHAPTER... ...FIVE

Zac started wriggling up the passage. It was a tight squeeze and he couldn't see any light ahead. But the tunnel was sloping upwards and to Zac's relief it wasn't long before he climbed back into the main passageway.

His SpyPad was on the ground near the edge of the hole. Zac grabbed it and checked the time.

It was already dawn and he was no closer to finding Agent Track Star. Suddenly, the ground trembled again. Zac covered his head as pebbles pelted down. They were becoming stronger. Zac had to hurry!

Zac tied his beetle-torch to his Pyramid-Pack as he hurried along. Ahead of him the corridor went off in two different directions. *Which way should I go?* There was no way he wanted to end up down another hole.

Then Zac saw something out of the corner of his eye. There was writing on the floor of the left-hand passage.

He shone the SpyPad's glowing screen at the spot but the word instantly vanished. Zac was puzzled for a moment. Then he had an idea. *Maybe whatever it is can only be seen with ultraviolet light.*

Zac shone the beetle-torch over the ground. Sure enough, stamped on the ground, was 'GIB'! *Agent Track Star must have used the GIB Invisible Stamp-pad to leave a clue!* It was a way for GIB agents to leave secret messages for each other.

Usually Zac had to turn on the ultraviolet screen in his SpyPad to see the invisible ink. But the beetle-torch was doing the same job. *Agent Track Star came this way,* thought Zac. *I must be on the right track.*

Zac shone the beetle-torch down the left-hand tunnel. More glowing marks appeared, leading all the way down.

*This mission just got a whole lot easier*, chuckled Zac.

He followed the marks for a while but then, quite suddenly, they stopped. The tunnel ended at the doorway of a small room. Zac looked in. On the back wall was a giant painting of a human with a cat's head. Zac took a step backwards. He was more of a dog person than a cat person. And there was something *very* dodgy about this cat.

Zac knew that a spy must always trust his gut instincts. He picked up a rock and rolled it into the middle of the room.

## ZZZᶻⱫZⱫZAPPPPPP!

A zap of light shot out of the cat's eye and blasted the pebble into a smoking pile of dust.

Being careful not to step any further into the room Zac held up his torch and took a better look at the painting. Over the cat's eye was something that looked like a glass marble cut in half.

*An ancient magnifying lens!* thought Zac.

He was pretty sure he knew what was going on. But he wanted to check. He rolled another rock into the room and watched carefully. When the rock fell into the cat's path a lever behind its eye flipped up. This

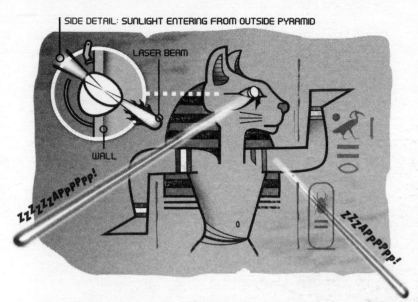

SIDE DETAIL: SUNLIGHT ENTERING FROM OUTSIDE PYRAMID

LASER BEAM

WALL

ZZZ-ZZZAPPPPP!

ZZZAPPPPP!

allowed a ray of sunlight to come through a hole behind the eye. When the sunbeam hit the magnifying glass, it acted like a laser beam. Anything that crossed its path would be instantly destroyed.

Zac was impressed. Of course, during the night it wouldn't work at all. But during daylight it was deadly.

Zac couldn't resist trying the laser out one more time. He took off his hat. It was the one his mum always made him wear in the sun. It was totally ugly and scratchy too. Zac flicked the hat into the room.

*Pffffffft!*

It disappeared into a puff of smoke.

Excellent!

After seeing the rocks and the hat blasted away there was no way Zac was going to risk walking in there. He needed a way of covering the cat's eye.

Zac felt in his pocket. He had a couple of paint bombs that would do the trick. But they would also wreck the wall-paintings and he didn't really want to do that. The paintings were old and faded but they were kind of cool too. Plus his mission was to *repair* damage, not make more.

So Zac pulled out some chewing gum and a rubber band instead. Perfect! Zac quickly chewed the gum into a ball and then flicked it across the room with the rubber band.

## Kerrrrrrrrrrr-SPLATTT!

Bullseye! The gum was now covering the magnifying lens. But Zac didn't have time to feel pleased with himself.

Every second counted.

He had to keep moving.

# CHAPTER SIX

Zac quickly walked through the Cat Room and out another door on the far wall. The passage continued for a bit and then Zac found himself in another room.

*Cool! The Mummy Room.*

Lying on a table in the middle of the room was a golden sarcophagus. Zac knew that this was a kind of coffin mummies were kept in. The room was cold. And really dark. In fact, it was kind of creepy. But Zac wasn't the type of kid who got scared. He especially wasn't the type to be scared of some old, dead mummy.

Suddenly Zac heard a banging noise.

It seemed to be coming from inside the sarcophagus! Most kids would probably have run away screaming at this point. But not Zac. *There must be a simple explanation,* he thought. *I'll just open up the sarcophagus and see what's inside.* But all the same his heart was beating hard as he walked towards the noise.

## *Crrrreeeak!*

The sarcophagus was very heavy to open. Inside was a figure about the same height as Zac, wrapped from head to toe in bandages.

Its arms rose up from its sides, like a zombie, and it moaned as it took a step towards him.

*It can't really be a mummy,* thought Zac. *I need to get those bandages off and see what — or who — is underneath.*

He reached into the Pyramid-Pack and his hand closed around something that felt like a can of fly spray. That wouldn't be much use. Zac checked the label. *Bandage-B-Gone,* it said. *Super strength instant bandage remover.* Leon had thought of everything when he put this Pyramid-Pack together!

Just as the mummy lurched towards

him, Zac sprayed
the figure with the
Bandage-B-Gone.

A massive cloud
instantly billowed
up in the air as the
bandages dissolved.
Zac heard coughing
coming from inside
the cloud.

'Who's there?' he asked, sharply. 'Show
yourself.'

'It's Agent Track Star,' came the reply.
Zac was puzzled. Agent Track Star didn't
sound how he was expecting him to sound.

When the cloud cleared Zac gasped at

what he saw. He now knew why Agent Track Star sounded different.

Agent Track Star was a girl!

'I got caught in a booby trap,' explained Agent Track Star when she stopped coughing. 'One minute I was walking along and the next thing I knew I was wrapped up in bandages inside that sarcophagus. Thanks for rescuing me. You must be Zac Power. I'm Caz.'

Zac looked at her suspiciously.

'What are you doing in here anyway? You were supposed to be guarding the pyramid from the outside,' he said.

'I thought I heard tomb raiders inside,' replied Caz. 'I decided to go in and save the Golden Sun Diamond.'

Suddenly Caz's eyes filled with tears. For a horrible moment Zac thought she might cry.

'But I can't do it on my own,' she said. 'I need help.'

'I'll help you,' said Zac. 'We're both GIB agents after all. We're *supposed* to help each other.' Caz smiled gratefully.

'Cool. Follow me,' she said. And she took off down a corridor.

Zac had little choice but to follow her.

There wasn't much time left.

He hoped Caz knew what she was doing. She led him down winding passageways and in and out of rooms, all at a really fast pace.

'You know your way around here pretty well,' Zac said. He was getting puffed trying to keep up.

'I'm the top scorer on *Pyramid Panic*,' said Caz proudly. 'I know this place backwards.'

Finally Caz stopped.

'This is the Treasure Room,' she said.

Zac gasped. Around the walls were piles of gold coins and sparkling jewels. Right in the middle was a giant statue with a lion's head. And in its hands was the biggest jewel Zac had ever seen. It was easily the size of a basketball.

'The statue is the Golden Sun King,' whispered Caz. 'And in his lap is the Golden Sun Diamond.'

'It's amazing it's never been stolen,' said Zac. Caz nodded.

'Yep, apparently there's some curse protecting it from thieves,' she said. 'It's said to be guarded by a huge army of scorpions…'

Just then, the floor rumbled again.

**RRRRRUMMMMBLE!**

This time it wasn't just pebbles that fell from the ceiling. It was rocks the size of Zac's fist! It felt like the pyramid was beginning to collapse.

'We've got to leave,' yelled Zac above the noise.

'No!' yelled back Caz. 'The diamond isn't safe in here. We must take it back to Headquarters.'

Zac looked at Caz. Although she was supposed to be a top spy she seemed like a little kid to Zac. *She doesn't even look strong enough to lift that diamond*, thought Zac. But she also seemed pretty stubborn. He could tell there was no way she was leaving without it.

'Let me get it,' Zac said, taking a step towards the statue.

Caz grabbed his arm.

'Look out!' she cried, pointing downwards. In front of Zac was a wide trench. Out of it was coming a strange hissing sound. Then a giant cobra, thicker than Zac's leg, rose up out of the trench. It stared at him with its black, beady eyes.

Seconds later another one appeared beside it.

Then another.

And another.

# CHAPTER
## ...SEVEN

Zac stood very still. He knew that the slightest movement would cause the cobras to strike. But the snakes hadn't seen Caz. She was hidden behind Zac.

'Caz,' Zac whispered. 'Get my iPod out of my Pyramid-Pack.' He felt Caz reach into the Pyramid-Pack and pull out the iPod.

'Now, find the album called *Music for Soothing Savage Beasts*,' Zac said, 'and plug it into my SpyPad so it plays through the speakers.'

'Which song?' whispered Caz.

'Track seven,' Zac replied. At least he *hoped* it was track seven. He held his breath.

For a terrible moment he thought the iPod's batteries had gone flat. But then the track started.

Phew! It was the right track after all: 'Snake Charming Song'. The moment the cobras heard the music they began swaying backwards and forwards, like fans at a rock concert.

'Nice work, Zac!' said Caz, looking impressed. 'Now, grab the diamond.'

Zac jumped across the cobra pit. The snakes paid no attention to him at all. Zac reached out to pick up the diamond. But then he stopped. He remembered what Caz had said about the curse. He didn't believe in that stuff, of course. All the same though, he couldn't help feeling that something wasn't right. But there was no time to worry about it.

Zac grabbed the diamond. Underneath was a big dark hole. Zac froze, waiting for something to happen. But nothing did. Zac relaxed. The curse was obviously just made up to scare people.

'Caz,' called Zac. 'I can't jump across the pit with this – I'm going to throw the diamond across. Do you think you can catch it?'

Caz nodded. So Zac threw the diamond. To his surprise Caz had no trouble catching it. In fact, she caught it with one hand and then twirled it on one finger. Then she shoved the diamond in her backpack.

'Thanks Zac,' she grinned. 'I'm off to HQ.'

'Hang on,' said Zac. 'We can go there together.'

Caz seemed different all of a sudden. She laughed. It was a nasty laugh.

'Oh, I'm not going to GIB's HQ,' she said. 'I work for BIG now. And I'm going to get a massive promotion when I come back with this diamond. Thanks for helping me steal it.'

BIG! Zac had heard about them. They were the most evil and devious spies in the business. Now it all made sense.

'You're a double agent!' exclaimed Zac.

'That's right,' smiled Caz. 'I've been pretending to work for GIB while all along I was spying for BIG. Well Zac, it's been fun but now I'm going to have to leave you alone with these snakes.'

'But I rescued you from the sarcophagus!' said Zac angrily. 'You'd still be stuck in there if I hadn't come along!'

'You didn't rescue me,' Caz sneered. 'I didn't become the top player on *Pyramid Panic* without learning where all the booby traps are! I only pretended to be trapped so you would feel sorry for me and help me steal the diamond. Why should *I* do the dangerous work when I could trick you into doing it instead?'

Zac stared at Caz in shock. He couldn't believe anyone could be so devious.

Caz pressed a button on the side of her

spy shoes and two lines of wheels dropped into position. The shoes were instantly transformed into rollerblades.

'Bye, Zac Power!' said Caz. 'You're not a bad spy. You're *almost* as good as me. Maybe you should join BIG too?'

'I'd never work for BIG,' said Zac angrily.

'That's too bad,' said Caz, shrugging. 'See you later, *loser!*' And she skated towards the door.

Zac checked the time.

Things were going terribly wrong. Caz was escaping with the Golden Sun Diamond and Zac knew it wouldn't be long before his iPod went flat. When the music stopped those cobras were going to attack him for sure. And then things got even worse.

Zac heard a low, rumbling sound.

At first he thought it was another earth tremor. But then he realised the sound was coming from the hole that the diamond had been covering!

In shock Zac watched as a giant scorpion scuttled out of the hole. It was twice the size of his hand! Another scorpion followed behind the first. And another.

**DANGER**

**WEAR SHOES AT ALL TIMES**

Then hundreds of scorpions came flooding out, like water from a burst pipe. Zac couldn't help noticing that their tails were already up in the sting position. And they were heading straight for him.

# CHAPTER... ...EIGHT

Zac tried to leap out of the way. But he was too late. The scorpions swarmed all over him. So Zac stood very still, hoping that they would think he was a rock.

The scorpions ran under his clothes and over his face. Their legs were very ticklish, but Zac didn't feel like laughing.

*It's only a matter of time before I get stung,* he thought.

He just hoped there was some anti-venom in the Pyramid-Pack. But to his amazement the scorpions ran right over him and out the door.

*They're chasing Caz!* realised Zac. *They know she's got the diamond!*

What should he do? *I could just wait until the scorpions catch her,* thought Zac. There was no way she could outrun that many angry, giant scorpions, not even on skates. The other option was to rescue her. If he did then she would have to admit that *he* was the better spy. And she'd have to apologise for calling him a loser!

Zac liked that idea. But how was he going to rescue her?

He checked his Track Changer sandals. Maybe there was an animal on that dial that could help him out.

Fox? No good.

Coyote? Nup.

Kangaroo? Bingo!

He switched the shoes to 'Kangaroo' and took an enormous jump.

**SPPPRRROOOOINGGGG!**

Zac leapt straight over the snake pit and took off down the passageway. It wasn't long before he could see Caz up ahead. She was skating fast, but the scorpions were catching up.

Zac jumped as hard as he could. Soon he was right behind the scorpions. Zac bent his knees. This next jump was going to have to be the biggest one he'd ever done.

**SPPPRRROOOOINGGGG!**

With an enormous jump Zac leapt over the swarm of scorpions and landed right behind Caz. He reached out and grabbed her backpack firmly in his hand. She jerked to a halt as he turned and jumped back over the scorpions.

'Hey!' yelled Caz angrily as she found herself pulled backwards through the air. 'What are you doing?'

'I'm rescuing you,' replied Zac. 'We have to return the diamond or you'll be stung by those scorpions.'

'There's no way I'm being rescued by you, Zac Power!' snarled Caz.

Still in mid-air she wiggled her arms out of the backpack and fell to the ground in a commando roll. She landed right in the path of the scorpions. But they scuttled right over the top of her without even stopping. They were after the bag with the diamond in it. And the bag was now in Zac's hand!

The walls began to shake again. They shook so much it was like the pyramid had suddenly been turned into jelly.

'Forget the diamond!' yelled Caz. 'This place is about to collapse. I'm outta here!' Then she skated off into the darkness.

Zac checked his watch as he bounced back towards the statue.

There was no time to chase Caz now. As much as he hated to do it, he would have to let her escape. He had to stick to his mission now and return the diamond.

Anyway, he had a feeling they would meet again.

# CHAPTER... ...NINE

The scorpions were close behind ... and were getting closer with every second! But Zac managed to stay just ahead of them.

A few bounces later he was back in the Treasure Room. Zac opened Caz's bag and yanked out the diamond. The statue was still a couple of leaps away, and the scorpions were closer than ever.

Zac skidded to a halt.

Blocking his path was the trench.

*The cobras!*

The iPod had stopped playing and one look at the snakes told Zac that they were no longer in a trance. In fact, they looked nastier than ever.

Zac thought fast. *I'll have to throw the diamond back over the snake pit and into the statue's lap. I'll just pretend I'm playing basketball.*

Zac was an excellent basketball player. But this was a high-pressure shot. Zac kept imagining Caz laughing at him. *You'll never make it*, she was saying in his mind.

But Zac ignored the voice. He had to make this shot. Sure, being a spy was a drag sometimes. But like it or not Zac Power was a GIB agent and he had a mission to complete. He took a deep breath and lined up the shot. Then he threw the diamond at the statue of the Golden Sun King.

From the moment it left his hands Zac realised he'd made a mistake. He'd thrown it way too hard! Of course, if he had been on the GIB basketball court this wouldn't have mattered. It would have just hit the backboard and bounced in but today there was no backboard for the diamond to bounce off.

There was just the statue's head.

## CRRRRACKKK!

The diamond hit the statue right in the

face. Zac held his breath, waiting to see what would happen next.

As if in slow motion the diamond rolled down the statue and into its hands. It wobbled there for a long moment. Zac could hardly watch. Would it stay put or would it end up rolling into the pit?

Finally, the diamond stopped wobbling. Zac leapt up in the air. Awesome shot! He just wished there was someone around to high-five.

The moment the diamond was safely back in its place the cobras disappeared into the trench and the scorpions ran straight past Zac and back down the holes in the walls. Zac wanted to breathe a sigh of relief. But he couldn't just yet. He had to check that the statue was OK.

From a distance the statue looked perfect. He put 'Snake Charming Song' back onto repeat and jumped over the pit. Up close Zac could see that there was a huge crack all the way around the statue's neck. When he pushed the head it fell off into his hands. *Oh no! I must have broken it with the diamond!*

Another earth tremor forced Zac to jump out of the way of the falling rocks. Zac coughed. His lungs were filling up with dust. He knew he should be finding a way out. But he didn't want to leave before he fixed the statue. It was going to be hard enough to explain to GIB about letting Caz escape. He didn't want to tell them that he'd wrecked this statue too.

Zac tipped his Pyramid-Pack upside down and shook it.

This was his last hope. Perhaps there was something in it that would be perfect for instantly fixing a broken statue.

The only thing to fall out of the bag was Zac's Super-Strength Hair Gel.

Zac felt his hair. It was still in perfect condition; even after all he'd been through. The hair gel was really strong stuff. *But is it strong enough to fix a 2000-year-old statue?* There was nothing for it but to try.

Zac quickly squeezed the tube of Super-Strength Hair Gel onto the statue's neck. Then he squished the head back on top.

To Zac's relief the gel set instantly. When he checked the head a moment later it was firmly stuck in place.

Zac smiled. There hadn't been a hair crisis yet that this gel couldn't solve!

The SpyPad beeped a warning.

Zac had seven minutes to get out. He turned around, ready to run for the door. But before he had a chance to escape, the pyramid shook again and a huge pile of rocks and sand came crashing down in front of him.

# CRRRRAAASHHHHHH!

When the dust cleared Zac couldn't see a tunnel any more.

He was trapped!

# CHAPTER TEN

There was no time for Zac to dig his way out. He was totally stuck! *Unless there's another way out?* thought Zac.

In a flash he remembered something else about *Pyramid Panic*. Whenever he played the game it was always the Treasure Room that he was ejected from.

He frowned, thinking hard. What caused him to be ejected? The only thing that he could remember was that he always seemed to trip over just before he found himself flying through the air.

The SpyPad had begun a warning countdown. Zac started pacing quickly around the room, looking for a clue.

Then suddenly he found himself sprawled on the ground. He'd tripped, just like when he played *Pyramid Panic*!

He looked down and saw two foot-prints carved into the stone he'd tripped on. The stone looked a bit like a welcome mat. But Zac knew that it was more like an *un*welcome mat.

Zac jumped on the stone and put his feet onto the carved footprints.

Immediately a panel in the ceiling creaked backwards and a light streamed through. It was so bright that at first Zac couldn't see anything.

Where was that light coming from? Then he realised. It was sunlight! This must be a tunnel leading up to the tip of the pyramid!

The stone beneath Zac's feet started pulling back slowly into the ground. Then suddenly it shot forward again, shooting Zac up into the air. Zac pressed his arms to his sides as he flew into the tunnel above his head. He couldn't stop smiling. This was wicked! He felt like a ball in a pinball machine.

When he opened his eyes again he was out in the sunshine, high above the pyramid.

Zac looked down at the pyramid. Was it going to collapse? That would be *really* annoying after all the effort he'd put into saving the statue.

The seconds ticked past but the pyramid didn't collapse. In fact, it remained as solid as it had for centuries. He'd made it out just in time!

The pyramid was saved!

Then Zac looked down again.

Uh oh! He remembered that what goes up, must come down. He was now hurtling towards the ground.

He could see his dune buggy far below him, looking like a toy. But it was getting bigger by the second. If he kept falling like this he was going to end up squashed like a bug on the windscreen.

Zac quickly thought back to what he had learned in Spy School about crash landing. He tucked his head down into his knees in the brace position.

Then he heard a strange noise. It was like a bird trying to flap its wings. It was coming from his Pyramid-Pack! There was the sound of ripping material and suddenly Zac wasn't falling any more.

In fact, he was gliding. Zac looked over his shoulder and smiled. There had been one last thing in his Pyramid-Pack that he hadn't noticed. A paraglider! The chute had opened up automatically as he started plummeting towards the ground.

*Now I can enjoy myself,* thought Zac. He did a couple of loop-the-loops and circled the pyramid below him before guiding the glider down towards the dune buggy. He pulled up in a perfect 10-point move and dropped right into the driver's seat.

Zac checked the solar power levels. The battery was completely charged again. He had more than enough energy to get back to base camp and meet up with his family. In fact, there was probably enough power to take the long way home and jump a few more sand dunes!

But there was one last thing he had to do. Zac untied the knot in the beetle-torch and let the scarab beetles out. In a flash they jumped off the buggy and burrowed down into the sand.

As Zac watched them disappear, the SpyPad's satellite phone rang.

'It's Agent Bum Smack here,' said a very familiar voice. 'Where are you, Zac? There's a big pile of dishes here at base camp. And according to the roster it's your turn to wash them.'

Zac sighed. It looked like the sand dunes would have to wait.

'OK, mum,' he said. 'I'm on my way.'

...**THE END**...

# EGMONT PRESS: ETHICAL PUBLISHING

Egmont Press is about turning writers into successful authors and children into passionate readers – producing books that enrich and entertain. As a responsible children's publisher, we go even further, considering the world in which our consumers are growing up.

**Safety First**
Naturally, all of our books meet legal safety requirements. But we go further than this; every book with play value is tested to the highest standards – if it fails, it's back to the drawing-board.

**Made Fairly**
We are working to ensure that the workers involved in our supply chain – the people that make our books – are treated with fairness and respect.

**Responsible Forestry**
We are committed to ensuring all our papers come from environmentally and socially responsible forest sources.

*For more information, please visit our website at*
*www.egmont.co.uk/ethicalpublishing*

For freebies, downloads
and other Zac Power info, go to

# www.zacpower.com